The Tales of
Olga da Polga

The Tales of
Olga da Polga

By MICHAEL BOND

Illustrated by HANS HELWEG

MACMILLAN PUBLISHING COMPANY
New York

Macmillan Publishing Company
866 Third Avenue, New York, NY 10022
First published by Penguin Books Ltd in Great Britain in 1971
First American Edition, 1973; reissued 1989
Printed in the United States of America

10 9 8 7 6 5 4 3 2 1

Library of Congress Cataloging-in-Publication Data
Bond, Michael.
The tales of Olga da Polga.
Summary: Recounts the adventures of an unusual
guinea pig that specializes in tall tales.
[1. Guinea pigs—Fiction] I. Helweg, Hans, ill. II. Title.
PZ7.B6368Tal 1989   [Fic]   88-31444
ISBN 0-02-711731-6

For Karen

Contents

The Tales of
Olga da Polga

1 · Olga Sets Out

From the very beginning there was not the slightest doubt that Olga da Polga was the sort of guinea pig who would go places.

There was a kind of charm about her, something in the set of her whiskers, an extra devil-may-care twirl to the rosettes in her brown and white fur, and a gleam in her eyes, which set her apart.

Even her name had an air of romance. How she had come by it was something of a mystery, and Olga herself told so many fanciful tales about moonlit nights, castles in the air, and fields awash with oats and beautiful princesses—each tale wilder than the one before—that none of the other guinea pigs in the pet shop knew what to believe.

1

However, everyone agreed that it suited her right to the very tips of her fourteen toes, and if some felt that it wouldn't come amiss if Olga was taken down a whisker or two it was noticeable none of them tried to do it, though many of them talked of the dangers of going out into the world alone, and without the protection of the humans who normally looked after them.

"You can't do without the *Sawdust People*," warned one old-stager known as Sale or Return, who'd lived in the shop for as long as anyone could remember and was always listened to with respect because he'd once been away for two whole days. "It's a cold, hard world outside."

But Olga would have none of it. "You can stay here if you like," she would announce, standing in the middle of the feeding bowl in order to address the others.

"But one of these days *I'm* going. Wheeeee! Just you wait. As soon as I see my chance I shall be away."

Olga was never quite sure whether she really believed her words or not, but she liked the sound of them, and secretly she also rather enjoyed the effect they had on the others.

Each night, before she settled down in the straw, she would look at her reflection in the water bowl, puffing out her cheeks and preening herself so that she would look her best if any likely looking customers came along.

And then it happened.

Quite unexpectedly, and not at all in the way Olga had always pictured it.

There were no grand farewells.

There was no battle royal.

No wild dash for freedom.

There were no cheers whatsoever.

In fact it was all over in a flash.

One morning, just as Olga was in the middle of her breakfast, a shadow fell across the cage and she looked up and saw a row of faces outside staring in at her.

There was the Sawdust Person she knew as the owner of the pet shop; a man she had never seen before; and a small girl.

It was the girl who caught Olga's gaze as she looked

3

up from the feeding bowl, and as their eyes met a finger came through the bars.

"That's the one," the girl said. "The one with the cheeky look and the oats sticking to her whiskers."

The door in the roof of the cage clanged open and a rough, hairy hand descended.

"She's yours for twenty-two and a half new pence," said the gruff voice of the pet-shop owner, grabbing hold of Olga. "To tell the truth I shan't be sorry to see the back of her. She's been a bit of a troublemaker ever since she came in."

Olga gave a squeak of outrage and alarm, and as she disappeared from view, kicking and struggling, some of the older guinea pigs nodded their heads wisely with an "I told you so" expression on their faces.

But many of the younger ones looked rather envious, for when your world is only two foot square almost anything else promises to be more exciting. Some of them were put off their food for the rest of the morning.

But if the other inhabitants of the pet shop wondered what was going on when Olga da Polga suddenly disappeared from view, Olga herself was in a dreadful state.

She didn't mind standing on an open and friendly hand once in a while, but it was quite a different matter being grabbed hold of and plonked—there was no other word for it—*plonked* into a cardboard box without so much as a by-your-leave.

Straight after a large breakfast too!

Her heart was beating like a tom-tom. Her dignity was shattered, her fur ruffled beyond description.

To cap it all she felt sick.

She had also made an important discovery. Going places when you know where you are going is one thing, but when you don't know it's quite a different matter.

For a moment or two she lay where she had landed, hardly daring to breathe. But after a while, opening first one eye and then the other, she cautiously took in her new surroundings.

It was dark, but there was a friendly smell of fresh

sawdust, and through a hole just above her head there came a shaft of light and a cooling draught of fresh air.

Olga had just begun to tell herself that perhaps things weren't so bad after all when, without any warning whatsoever, the box rose into the air and began jiggling up and down in a most alarming manner.

And as it tipped first one way and then another Olga began to wish she hadn't been so boastful in the past in case it was some kind of punishment. Old Sale or Return had often gone on about the way humans behaved and how strict they could be. Olga had always thought it was sour grapes because he'd been "returned" by one, but now she wasn't quite so sure.

There was worse to follow, for just as she was in the middle of trying to work out how many times she *had* actually boasted or told a story which wasn't exactly "true," the jiggling stopped; there was a roar, and a strange tickling began to run through her body, starting in her toes and ending where her tail would have been had she owned one.

"Oh, dear! Oh, dear!" she wailed. "Whatever's happening now?"

And then in a flash it came to her.

The noise, the tickling, the feeling that she was going somewhere even though she herself wasn't moving . . . it could only mean one thing.

"A motor car!" she exclaimed, jumping up and down with excitement. "I'm in a motor car!"

Olga knew all about motor cars because she'd seen them through the pet shop window, but never in her wildest dreams had she ever pictured herself *riding* in one.

Gathering her courage in both paws she clambered up the side of the box and by standing on tiptoe managed to peer through the hole above her head.

Of the houses and shops she'd grown up with there was no sign. Instead, all she could see was green countryside, miles and miles of it.

Fields, hedges, trees, banks covered with luscious-looking dandelions and thick, mouth-watering grass, all flashed past with the speed of the wind.

"If this is the outside world I've heard so much about," decided Olga, "I think I shall like it. It's much, much better than a stuffy, crowded old pet shop."

7

Then she pricked up her ears, for above the noise of the engine she caught the sound of voices. First a deep one, then another, much younger, which she recognized as belonging to the little girl who'd picked her out from among all the others.

"You'll have to look after her, Karen," said the deep voice. "Come rain or shine. No excuses."

"I promise." The second voice paused for a moment and then went on. "I do hope she likes her new home."

"She'd better," came the reply. "It cost me enough to build. What with the wood and the roofing felt, glass for the bedroom window, wire netting for the door, legs to keep her away from Noel . . ."

As the man's voice droned on Olga sank back onto the floor, hardly daring to believe her ears. "I'm going to stay with some Sawdust People," she breathed. "All by myself!

"And in a waterproof house with a bedroom," she added dreamily, "on *legs*.

"Why, I must be going to live in a palace. I really must!"

2 · The Naming of Olga da Polga

If Olga da Polga's new home wasn't exactly a palace it certainly seemed like it, and it was definitely the nearest she was ever likely to get to one.

After the cramped and crowded conditions in the pet shop it was like entering a different world.

The hutch was large and airy and it was divided into two halves. Both floors were neatly covered with sawdust and the rooms were separated by a wall which had a hole cut in the middle so that she could easily pass between the two.

The first half was a kind of all-purpose room; part dining room, part playroom; with a wire mesh door, a small ash branch in one corner so that she could keep her teeth nice and sharp, and two heavy bowls— one marked OATS and the other marked WATER.

Olga tried out both before turning her attention to the second room. This turned out to be even more exciting than the first, for it not only had a *glass window* to keep out the weather but there was a large, inviting mound of fresh-smelling hay as well.

Olga spent some time pressing the hay flat so that she would have somewhere comfortable to sleep without being too hot, and then she settled down to think things over.

Really, all things considered, life had taken a very pleasant turn.

The sun was shining. The birds were chirping. Even the noises seemed friendly; the clinkings, singing, and

occasional humming sounds from somewhere inside the big house as Mr. and Mrs. Sawdust—which was what Olga had decided to call them—went about their work.

Every so often there was a reassuring murmur of voices outside as one or other of the family peered through the glass to make certain she was all right.

First came Mr. Sawdust, then Mrs. Sawdust, then some other people called "neighbors" and they all had a friendly word or two to say to her.

Finally Karen Sawdust herself arrived with an enormous pile of grass, a bunch of dandelions, and a large juicy carrot neatly sliced down the center, which she placed temptingly alongside the feeding bowl.

"We're going to choose a name for you now," she announced, as Olga stirred herself and came out of the bedroom to sample these new delicacies. "And we have to make sure it's right because tomorrow Daddy's going to paint it over your front door. There'll be no changing it once that's done."

Olga nibbled away, half listening, half in a world of her own.

"Daddy fancies Greta and Mummy's rather keen on Gerda, but I'm not sure. They don't sound *special* enough to me." Karen Sawdust put her face against the door as she turned to go. "I do wish you could tell us what *you* would like for a name."

11

"Greta? . . . Gerda? . . . *Painted on my front door?*"
Olga's world suddenly turned upside down.

She paused, a carefully folded piece of grass half in,
half out of her mouth, hardly able to believe her ears.

"But I'm Olga da Polga," she wailed, addressing the
empty air. "I've always been Olga da Polga. I can't
change now—I really can't." That night, long after

darkness fell and everyone else had gone to bed, Olga
was still wide awake and deep in thought.

"I suppose," she said to herself, for what seemed like
the hundredth time, "I suppose I ought to be counting

my blessings instead of grumbling. I mean . . . I have a nice new home . . . food . . . I'm among friends . . . but I *would* like to keep my own name, especially as I'm having it painted on."

The more Olga thought about it the sadder she became, for she couldn't help remembering a remark one of the older inhabitants of the pet shop had once made. "Always hang on to your name," he had said. "It may not be much, but when you're a guinea pig it's sometimes all you have in the world."

Olga's own name was firmly imprinted on her mind. OLGA DA POLGA.

It had taken her fancy straight away and now she had become so used to it she couldn't begin to picture having anything else. When she closed her eyes she could still see it written in large black letters on the side of an old cardboard box.

Suddenly she jumped up in excitement, her mind in a whirl. Could she? Was it possible? She felt herself trembling at the sheer audacity of the idea.

It would mean a lot of hard work. A lot of difficult, almost impossible work. And yet . . .

Getting out of her warm bed, shivering partly with the chill of the night air and partly with she knew not what, Olga made her way through into the next room.

Clutching the ash branch firmly in her mouth she

set to work. Scratching and scraping, starting and stopping, she worked and she worked and she worked.
Sometimes pausing to smooth the sawdust over before
beginning all over again, she tried not once, but time
after time and still it wouldn't come right.

Dawn was breaking before she crawled back into
her bedroom at long last and sank down in the hay.
Her paws were aching, her fur was covered in sawdust,
and her eyes were so tired she could hardly bear to
keep them open.

"It looks plain enough to me," she thought, gazing
back at the result of her night's work, "but then, I
know what it's meant to be. I only hope the others
understand as well."

Gradually, as she enjoyed her well-earned rest, the
air began to fill with sounds of morning. Strange, un-
accustomed sounds. In place of the usual grunts and
rustles of the pet shop there were dogs barking, clocks

striking, the sound of bottles clinking, and somewhere in the distance the noise of a train rattling on its way. In fact, there were so many different noises Olga soon lost count of them.

And then, at long last, came the one she had been waiting for. There was a click, the clatter of a bolt being withdrawn, and a moment later a now familiar face appeared on the other side of the wire netting.

In the pause which followed Olga could almost hear the beating of her own heart.

"Mummy! Mummy!" With a shriek of surprise the face vanished from view. "Come quickly! Come and see!"

Olga jumped to her feet. "Wheeeee! It's worked! It's worked! Wheeeeeeee!" Squeaking with joy and pleasure at her own cleverness she ran round and round her dining room, scattering sawdust and the result of her labors in one wild whirlwind of delight.

"Olga da Polga?" exclaimed the voice of Mrs. Sawdust. "Written on the floor? Don't be silly . . . how *could* it have been?"

A face appeared at Olga's door. "I can't see anything at all. You must have been dreaming.

"All the same"—there was a pause—"it *is* rather a nice name. If I were you I'd keep it."

When they were alone again Olga looked out of her window at Karen Sawdust and Karen Sawdust looked back at her.

"Grownups!" said Karen with a sigh. "They *never* understand these things. Still, we know it happened, don't we?"

Olga da Polga lifted up her head proudly. "Wheeee!" she cried, in the loudest voice she could possibly manage. "Wheeee! Wheeeee! Wheeeeeeeee!"

And really, there was nothing more to be said.

3 · Olga Takes a Bite

Olga was so worn out after her night's work that straight after breakfast she went back to bed, and she slept and she slept and she slept.

She vaguely remembered waking once to a rather strange smell, but it turned out to be Mr. Sawdust doing something to the outside of her house so she promptly went back to sleep again. He'd been using what looked like a tiny tail on the end of a stick, which he kept dipping in a tin full of black stuff.

Whatever it was everyone seemed very pleased with the result, for they kept repeating her name, which was all very comforting.

Olga had no idea how long she stayed asleep after that, but it must have been quite some time, for when she finally woke, the sun, which had been on the bedroom side of her house at breakfast time, was now shining through her front door.

She stirred gently, stretched, scratched a few remaining grains of sawdust from her fur, shook herself, and then sat very still as a strange feeling came over her that she was BEING WATCHED.

She peered out of her window and then hurried to the front door, but there wasn't a soul in sight.

Taking a few nibbles from a lettuce leaf, she helped herself to an oat or two for good measure and was about to settle down again when it happened.

Glancing up for no better reason than the fact that it made a change from looking down she caught sight of a strange, upside-down face watching her from the top of the hutch. Worse still, a moment later a long, black object, like a piece of furry rope, slid into view and began swinging lazily to and fro.

Left . . . right, left . . . right, it went . . . just like the pendulum of a clock, brushing against the wire mesh door, not more than an inch from her nose. If it hadn't been for the fact that every so often it paused, as if to show it was capable of other things, and gave a flick in the opposite direction, the motion might well have sent Olga off to sleep again.

She watched it for a moment or two longer and then came to a decision.

18

There was only one way of telling if both head and object belonged to the same creature and she took it.

Biding her time, she waited until it made one of its sudden changes in direction, curling for a brief moment through one of the holes in the wire, then she made a dive.

As Olga sank her twenty teeth into the offending object it was wrenched from her grasp and a loud high sound of mingled pain and alarm echoed round the garden.

The yowling and howling that followed as both face and object disappeared from view was enough to wake the dead.

It certainly brought the Sawdust family running.

Doors banged. Voices called out. Feet clattered . . .

Olga watched with growing interest as first one member of the family and then another ran past her house.

"I don't know who or what it was," she thought, "but start as you mean to go on—that's what I always say." And she went back to her oats.

"Kutchy, kutchy, kutchy . . . come on down. Kutchy, kutchy, kutchy."

"Goodness knows what frightened him so."

"Come on down . . . kutchy, kutchy."

"WRETCHED ANIMAL!"

The voices began to grow more and more impatient.

Mr. Sawdust hurried back past Olga's house, only to return a few minutes later, red in the face and breathing heavily, as he struggled beneath the weight of an enormous wooden object about twice as long as he was tall.

"I've had to borrow an extending ladder from next door," he called. "We'll never reach him otherwise."

"An *extending ladder!*" Olga grew more and more interested. She had no idea what it meant but it sounded most exciting.

"I must do this more often," she thought. "It's a fine way to pass the time on a summer's evening." And she hurried round her house taking bites out of anything that happened to get in her way.

But the others didn't seem to share Olga's enthusiasm.

Cries of "Be careful!" and "Mind you don't slip!" floated up from the garden.

It seemed that the object Olga had bitten was now sitting at the top of a very tall pine tree and there was even talk of fetching something called a Fire Brigade.

But to Olga's disappointment, for she had never seen a Fire Brigade, let alone been the cause of having one fetched, just as the excitement and Mr. Sawdust had both reached their highest point, the object took it into its head to come down again by itself.

"Cats!" said Mr. Sawdust bitterly.

There was a banging and clattering and a moment or so later he came past Olga's house again, still carry-

21

ing the ladder, and looking even more red in the face than before.

"Noel, you naughty thing!" Karen Sawdust came into view carrying a very cowed and frightened-looking bundle of black fur in her arms. "I don't know what Olga will think of you. Why can't you be good like her?"

There was no knowing what Olga thought of Noel, for she appeared to be much too busy munching her oats to bother with looking up, but it was only too clear what Noel thought of Olga. As he was placed on the ground he arched his back and his fur bristled and he glared at the hutch with a "just you wait" expression on his face.

Olga looked down at him haughtily. "Wheeeeee!" she squeaked, from the safety of her dining room. "You can't frighten me. My house has legs to keep me safe from you. Mr. Sawdust told me. He went to great expense."

Noel gave a kind of hissing snort. "Legs are meant for climbing," he said menacingly. "So just you wait. One of these days I'll bite your tail so hard it'll . . ." He broke off and stared as Olga turned her back on him.

"You . . . you haven't got a tail!" he exclaimed.

"No," said Olga primly. "I haven't."

"But all furry animals have tails," said Noel.

Olga turned round again to face him. "Guinea pigs haven't," she replied. "That's what makes us different."

She paused, a thoughtful gleam in her eye as she felt another sort of tale coming on. "We lost them a long, long time ago," she said with a sigh. "If you like, I'll tell you just how it happened. It's really rather romantic."

4 · Olga's Story

"Once upon a time," said Olga, who, if she wasn't yet sure of what her story would be about, at least knew how it should start. "Once upon a time, guinea pigs had the most marvelous tails imaginable. Long and thick, with fur like silky cream. If you can picture a great long yarn of the finest silk . . ."

"A great long yarn is right," interrupted Noel with a yawn. "*Do* get on with it. I don't want to hang around here all night. I have work to do."

"I'm only telling you all this," said Olga coldly, "because I don't want you to get the wrong idea. I wouldn't like you to confuse guinea pigs' tails, as they were then, with any ordinary sort of tail—like a *cat's,* for instance."

She paused, partly for effect, but mostly to think up what to say next.

"Have you ever heard of Peru?" she inquired hopefully. "That's where we guinea pigs first came from."

"I've heard of it," said Noel, not wishing to sound too ignorant. "I've never *been* there."

"Oh!" Olga looked slightly taken aback. "Er . . . well I don't suppose for a moment you've ever heard of Barsance," she said, using the first word that came into her head. "It's so small no one has *ever* heard of it." And she glared at Noel as if to dare him to say he had.

"Barsance used to be joined on to Peru," she continued, "until one night when there was a terrible storm and it broke off.

"It was so small that at the time I'm talking about, which was long, long ago, there was only room for one of everything.

"There was one king who ruled over a kingdom which had only one house with one inhabitant.

"This king lived with his stepdaughter in a one-roomed castle perched on an enormous rock overlooking the village, and he was known far and wide as the most crotchety and bad-tempered old king there had ever been.

"But it was said by the few who'd seen his stepdaughter that she was the most beautiful princess in

25

the whole world; as beautiful as he was ugly, and as sweet as he was unkind and selfish."

Olga stared dreamily into space as she began to be carried away by her own story. "Her eyes . . ."

"Did she have more than one eye?" asked Noel eagerly.

"Her eyes," said Olga firmly, "were so beautiful that when you gazed into them it was like looking into *one* very still lake of the deepest blue you could possibly imagine.

"But they were sad eyes, for her stepfather was very jealous of her beauty and never allowed anyone near the castle in case they took her away.

"Each morning when she woke she looked at herself in the mirror and gave a sigh as she thought of all the wonderful things that might have happened had she been a normal princess living in a land where there was more than one of everything.

"And then she would retire to the one tower the castle possessed and sit gazing dreamily out of the one window in the hope that one day she would be rescued.

"It wasn't a very tall tower, for it needed only one step to reach it, but the rock on which the castle stood was sheer as a cliff and tall as a mountain, and the castle itself could only be reached across a single draw-bridge and by climbing a tunnel hollowed out inside the rock. It was so tall that even the one eagle which inhabited the land of Barsance seldom rose above it, but spent most of its time swooping and soaring in the valley below.

"As time went by it seemed to the princess that she would never be rescued.

"And then one day a tall stranger rode into the village on horseback and inquired of the only inhabitant about the beautiful princess he'd heard tell of in distant lands.

"The man directed the stranger to the castle, but when the king saw him approach he flew into a terrible rage, and raised the drawbridge as he sent him packing. And in his temper he locked the heavy oak doors and hurled the key far out into space so that it was lost for ever.

"The prince was beside himself with grief, for in the short time he'd been at the castle he'd caught sight of the princess sitting alone in the tower and he realized that all the things he'd heard tell of her were true. And hadn't she waved? And hadn't he caught the sound of her voice calling out to him for help?

" 'Oh, if only I could rescue her,' he cried. 'If only I had wings so that I could fly up and take her away with me.'

"He gazed up at the rock, but it was polished

smooth as glass and by its side the one small rope he was able to find in the village was like a matchstick compared to the tallest pine.

"Time after time, feet slipping, fingers torn and bleeding, he tried to scale the rock, but it was no use. With a sinking heart he realized that not only would he never reach his loved one but that even if he went for help by the time he returned she might be dead, for without the key there was no getting in or out of the castle.

"Suddenly he felt he was being watched, and when he turned he found to his surprise what seemed like a million pair of eyes staring at him across the border from Peru.

"Peru," said Olga, for Noel's benefit, "was full of guinea pigs at the time for it was before we'd been discovered.

"One of these guinea pigs stepped forward. 'Tell us,' he said to the prince, 'what are you doing?'

"The prince sat down wearily and told his story. The guinea pigs listened with sorrow, for they knew the princess well and thought highly of her. Unlike her stepfather, who was forever driving them away and shouting at them, she always had a kind word to spare or a tasty tidbit to drop down from her tower.

"When the prince had finished his story the guinea pigs disappeared for a while and there was a strange rushing sound, like a gathering wind, as they whispered together. And then there were squeaks and grunts the like of which had never been heard before in the whole of Peru, let alone the kingdom of Barsance.

"At last they returned, dragging behind them a long, silky rope.

"At a signal from their leader the eagle came swooping down out of the sky, took hold of one end of the rope, and flew up to the princess waiting high above.

"With the rope securely tied round the bars, it took the prince only a matter of moments to climb up to the tower and even less time than it takes to tell before he was back down again with the princess at his side.

"He lifted her onto his horse and then, as he turned to thank all those present for their trouble, he suddenly realized the great and noble sacrifice they had made in his honor. For each and every guinea pig had given up its tail so that it might be woven into the rope which had saved the princess.

"The prince could think of no way to repay the guinea pigs for their act of kindness, so intead he bestowed on them the highest award he could think of.

"Not simply a medal—which would be very difficult to pin on and might fall off and be lost—but a rosette to be worn on their fur and on the fur of those who came after them until the end of time."

Olga turned round and looked at her own rosettes, "Which is why," she said, "if you are a guinea pig with a rosette it's very likely you are a direct descendant of those very same guinea pigs who gave their tails away all those years ago."

Olga felt so moved by her story

that a lump came into her throat and for a moment or two she found it quite difficult to swallow her oats.

Noel thought for a moment. "I don't think I'd give up *my* tail for a princess," he said bluntly, "however beautiful she was."

"Guinea pigs happen to have generous natures," said Olga. "Not like cats."

"If you're so generous," said Noel, "how about letting me have a piece of your grass before I go out for the night?"

But Olga was fast asleep. Telling tales could be very tiring. Especially tales about tails.

Besides, she'd had quite enough of cats for one day.

5 · Olga Makes a Friend

Olga soon settled down as one of the family. She loved her new home and it was nice to hear her name being called each morning at breakfast time.

She also made quite a number of new friends. Other guinea pigs were brought along by their owners to say hello, not to mention several rabbits, a hamster, two budgerigars and a collection of mice.

Really, life was very pleasant.

If she had a complaint at all, and she wouldn't have dreamed of mentioning it even if she had been able to, it was that during the middle of the day her house often grew a little too warm for comfort. Often she secretly wished she could romp and dance on the lawn she was able to see through her bedroom window, for it was shaded by a large tree and looked very cool and inviting.

Then one morning she was wakened by a strange new sound. Saw . . . saw . . . saw. Bang . . . bang . . . bang. It was most disturbing and it showed no sign of stopping.

Suddenly, just when she thought the worst was over, the door of her cage opened and she found herself being picked up and placed inside a strange, tall, upside-down affair, half hutch, half wooden frame covered on three sides by wire netting.

No sooner had she settled down to inspect her new surroundings than someone took hold of the contraption and turned it over.

Olga had to scramble like mad in order to keep her footing and when she finally recovered she found herself staring out at a kind of long, bottomless cage.

"Really!" she thought. "Whatever next? If this is progress I don't think much . . ." She paused and looked out from the platform on which she was standing.

She looked first at the sea of faces pressed against the side of the wire netting and then at the place where the floor ought to have been.

"How nice," said Karen Sawdust, "to have a daytime run where you really can eat off the floor."

"Safe from other animals," added Mrs. Sawdust.

"It'll help keep the grass short as well," said Mr. Sawdust. "If she works hard I shan't need to cut it any more!"

Olga looked up. She was a polite guinea pig and she felt it would be nice to say "thank you," but words failed her.

Besides, she was a firm believer in the old guinea pig saying that "a piece of clover in the mouth is worth two on the lawn," and having just found a particularly juicy clump her mouth was very, very full.

From that day on Olga spent most of her waking hours on the lawn. If she didn't exactly manage to keep the whole of it short it wasn't for want of trying, and Mr. Sawdust made sure that when he did use the mower he always left a corner uncut especially for her. It seemed as if every day was made up of sunshine and grass, and life could hardly have been sweeter.

It was on just such a day that Olga met Fangio.

It was late one afternoon. Karen Sawdust was at a place called school. Mr. Sawdust was at another place called work, and Mrs. Sawdust was busy indoors with her house.

Apart from Noel, who was chasing a fly in a nearby patch of heather, there was no sign of life whatsoever, and the only new object on the horizon was a kind of prickly round ball at the other end of the lawn.

Olga first noticed the ball when she was doing the rounds of her run clearing up the odd blades of grass before she was moved on to the next patch, and she

was about to go round for the second time when she paused.

The ball wasn't in the same place! Without anyone kicking it, or even touching it, it had moved. It *definitely* wasn't where it had been the first time she saw it.

Noel gave her a superior look when she told him of her discovery. "That's not a *ball*," he said. "That's Fangio. He lives in a garage down the road and they do say he has Argentine blood. He's a hedgehog."

"A *hedgehog?*" repeated Olga. "With Argentine blood? Wheeeee! What will they think of next?"

Fangio went past Olga's run several times, looking at her out of the corner of his eye, before he finally spoke. "Who are you?" he asked suspiciously. "I haven't seen you around before."

"I'm a hedgehog-eater from Upper Burma!" Olga had a large stock of such words, most of which she'd seen written on the sides of boxes. She kept them for use on special occasions and this seemed to be one of

them. "Wheeeeee!" she cried, in as loud and fierce a voice as she could possibly manage.

Fangio scuttled away and disappeared into the undergrowth.

He was gone some while and when he returned he looked at Olga even more suspiciously. "You're not a hedgehog-eater at all," he said. "I've been making inquiries. You're a guinea pig. You tell tales."

"Sometimes," said Olga carelessly, taking another nibble. "When I feel in the mood and the sun is in the right direction."

Fangio considered the matter for a monent. "I could tell a few tales if I liked," he said. "All about the Elysian Fields. That's where I'm off to now. I go there every evening."

"The Elysian Fields?" Olga stopped eating. In spite of herself she couldn't help feeling interested. "What are they when they're at home?"

"They're not *at home*," said Fangio. "That's the

whole point." He nodded vaguely in the direction of the shrubbery. "They're over there. I can't think why you bother to stay cooped up in a cage when there's so much else to see. The world's a big place you know, and it's full of interesting things."

"I'm happy where I am, thank you very much," said Olga smugly. "I have my run and plenty to eat. And I have a house on legs with a dining room and a bedroom with a window to look out of."

"I carry *my* windows with me," said Fangio, blinking his beady eyes. "And if I were to tell you some of the things I've seen through them it would make your fur stand on end."

"I like my fur the way it is, thank you," said Olga. "Er . . . what things?"

"Trees," said Fangio. "Bushes, banks, leaves, rubbish dumps, bonfires, roads, lanes, vegetables, flora and fauna, copses, green meadows, mushrooms, ponds, streams, the springiest turf you could possibly imagine, puddles, strange insects, pheasants' eggs, hay, straw, mollusks, worms, shady nooks, holes in the ground . . . I could go on all night but I've so much to do I really can't spare the time.

"If I were you I'd be up and away. I wouldn't spend *my* life at the beck and call of others. I'd *do* things. Stand on my own four paws for a change.

"Think of it . . . instead of having to wait every day until someone feeds you, you could do it yourself. Eat when *you* feel like it. What you like, *when* you like. They don't call it the Elysian Fields for nothing."

"They've never forgotten me yet," said Olga dubiously.

"Ah," said Fangio darkly, "but supposing they did? Suppose one day they weren't there and you were left shut up in your house . . ."

"Is it very dangerous in these fields?" asked Olga.

Fangio snorted. "Dangerous? *Dangerous?* If anything comes along I don't like the look of I just roll myself up into a ball and wait until they go away again. There's nothing to it. I'd like to see the animal that would frighten me."

"Even dogs?" asked Olga, who'd once seen a very large one from up the road. It was called an Alsatian and she hadn't liked the look of it at all.

"Dogs?" Fangio jumped. "What? Where?"

"A great big one," said Olga, making the most of it. "Foaming at the mouth, with fangs as big as cucumbers . . . I'll tell you a story about it if you like . . ."

But Fangio had gone. Moving with a surprising turn of speed for his size he'd vanished into the nearby bushes as if his very life depended on it.

Olga sat staring at the spot for quite a while. Somehow she felt strangely unsettled and the grass which she'd been enjoying up until a minute or so before now seemed dull and tasteless.

It was not a very nice feeling and try as she might she couldn't shake it off.

"I do hope Olga's all right," said Karen Sawdust later that evening after she'd put her to bed. "She seemed very odd. Not at all her usual self."

"I shouldn't worry, dear," said her mother. "I expect guinea pigs have their 'off days' just as we do."

And really she couldn't have spoken a truer word. For although Olga might not be having an "off day" at that very moment she definitely had the thought on her mind, and as she closed her eyes and made ready for sleep she decided to have one just as soon as she possibly could.

6 · Olga's Day Off

In her heart of hearts Olga didn't really expect to go roaming for quite some time, if at all, so she was doubly surprised when the opportunity came the very next day. Like most opportunities it happened unexpectedly, so that she had to make her decision at once before it passed her by.

In moving her run, someone—she wasn't sure who it was, for she was much too busy to notice—someone had been very careless and placed one corner of it on top of a small mound of grass. And this left a gap several inches high along part of one side.

Such a thing had never happened before and probably never would again. So Olga was left with no choice: It was now or never.

As soon as she felt she was alone she eased herself gently under the wooden frame, lowering her back and stretching herself out as far as she could, and suddenly she found herself on the other side.

She stood for a moment or two getting her breath back. All sorts of curious feelings were racing around inside her; part excitement, part fear, part elation at having done something so daring.

Even the air seemed different on the other side of her wire fence. Fresher somehow, and cleaner; full of the unknown.

Now she was ready for the big moment. The one she had been waiting for. The one she had dreamed about. She could start on her travels.

Which way should she go? Really, with the world at her feet and on every side as well it was hard to make a choice.

First of all she decided against the long, winding path leading back toward the house. There was no sense in risking capture quite so soon.

Then there was a vegetable patch nearby, full of tempting cabbage leaves and lettuce plants, but she ruled this out too, for Mr. Sawdust sometimes worked there and she might easily be spotted.

She wondered what Fangio would have done. Where was it he said he went to? The Elysian Fields? They

couldn't be that far away. Not if he went there every evening.

Olga's mouth, which had been unusually dry until a moment ago, began to grow moist with anticipation at the thought of the good things to come.

"Wheeeeee!" she squeaked. "This is the life!" And without wasting any more time she bounded across the lawn in a series of short, sharp bursts until she found herself in the shrubbery!

Although she wouldn't have admitted it, even to herself, Olga found the shrubbery a trifle disappointing. From a distance it had always looked most inviting, with shady nooks and branches which waved gently in the breeze as if beckoning any passerby to pause awhile and sample the delights within.

But far from its being full of delights Olga found it rather mucky, and very overgrown; chock-a-block with weeds and sharp brambles which parted easily enough but then immediately swung back again, cutting off her return with a dense barrier of thorns.

The further she went in, the worse it became. Pushing, shoving, scrambling over dead twigs and branches, Olga forced her way deeper and deeper into the undergrowth.

It was all very well for Fangio. He had prickles to start off with. A few more were probably neither here

nor there. But for a guinea pig with only her fur to protect her—fur, moreover, which she'd always prided herself on keeping neat and clean—it was quite a different matter.

Halfway through the shrubbery Olga's fur already looked as if it had been dragged through a hedge backwards, and by the time the first few chinks of light appeared on the other side she hardly dared look down at herself for fear of what she might see.

At last, battered and bruised, scratched and ruffled, she burst through the remaining mass of tangled foliage and lay panting with exhaustion while she took stock of her new surroundings.

"Elysian Fields indeed!" she exclaimed bitterly.

As far as she could make out, Fangio's heaven on earth was nothing more than a rubbish dump, full of old tin cans and soggy bits of cardboard, and smelling strongly of bonfires.

As for food! Olga didn't really count two mangy-looking thistles and a bed of old nettles as being fit for a compost heap let alone a hungry guinea pig.

As she contemplated it she grew gloomier and gloomier.

And at that moment, as if to add to her sorrows, it began to rain. First one spot, then another, then several more. Ping . . . ping . . . ping, ping, ping, they went on the old tin cans.

Then faster still, and harder. Rat-tat-tat-tat-tat.

The spots became a downpour, the downpour a deluge. The burning embers of the bonfire sizzled out leaving behind an acrid smell. The nettles drooped beneath the weight. Trees added their drips to the cascade of water.

Olga made a dive for a nearby sheet of cardboard and sat shivering beneath it. Never, in all her life, had she felt so wet and miserable, so . . .

There was a rustle from somewhere nearby and a

47

moment later a familiar head poked out from beneath
some leaves.

"Enjoying yourself?" asked Fangio. "Having fun?"

"*Enjoying* myself?" Olga stared at Fangio. "Having
fun?" she repeated. "I've never so unenjoyed myself in
the whole of my life! If this is the Elysian Fields the
sooner I'm back on my lawn the better! I've never
seen anything so . . . so dismal!"

"Beauty," said Fangio, "is in the eye of the beholder. I must say that through *my* windows it looks lovely. Think of all the flies and insects there'll be when it stops raining."

Olga shuddered. Fangio was welcome to his insects. She hadn't the slightest wish to stay and see them. "If you ask me," she said, "*your* windows need cleaning. Good night!"

"Second on the right," called Fangio, as Olga stalked off, taking the long way home round the outside of the shrubbery. "Third on the left, then right again. Only mind you don't fall in the . . . oh!"

He broke off as an extra-loud splash sounded above the rain.

"You might have told me!" wailed Olga, as she clambered out of a mud-filled hole.

"You didn't give me a chance," said Fangio.

"Hedgehogs!" snorted Olga bitterly.

She had never felt so glad to see her run. Nor, for that matter, had she had such a welcome before. Judging by the whoops of delight that greeted her reappearance, it seemed as if everyone in the neighborhood had been out looking for her.

"How nice to be back home," she thought. "How I could ever have wanted to leave I don't know."

"Where *have* you been?" cried Karen Sawdust, as she gathered Olga up in her arms. "We've been searching everywhere."

Mr. Sawdust held up an umbrella for protection.

"Pooh!" said Mrs. Sawdust. "She smells of bonfires."

Olga took a deep breath. "I've been to the Elysian Fields," she squeaked. "And I'm never, *ever* going there again!"

At least, that's what she meant to say, and if the squeaks themselves didn't exactly make sense to everyone around, the feeling that went into them made the meaning very clear indeed.

7 · Olga Wins a Prize

After her dreadful experience in the Elysian Fields Olga decided it was high time she settled down for a while. She even invented a slogan, MORE EATING—LESS THINKING, and spent long hours outside in her run making up for the weight she felt sure she must have lost.

She always inspected her run very carefully each morning, making certain that there was no possible way in for any other creature, and that she herself couldn't get out by mistake either, but so much care was now taken over the placing of her run that there was hardly room for a centipede to crawl under the edge let alone a guinea pig with a hearty appetite.

And then one day something unusual happened.

Hearing voices approach she hurried into the enclosed portion of the run in order to brace herself between the wooden floor and the back while it was turned on end. However, instead of being taken back home in the usual fashion, she found herself being carried into the big house where the Sawdust family lived.

She was taken through the kitchen, along a passage, and into a big room, where she was placed on top of a thing called a "table," a large area of very slippery wood high off the ground, with NO SIDES WHATSOEVER.

Olga knew all this because Karen Sawdust, who had been carrying her, explained matters as they went along.

She sat very still, hardly daring to move, while everyone gathered round and began prodding, poking, staring, and even—biggest indignity of all—TURNING HER UPSIDE DOWN!

Olga was most upset. "How would *they* like it," she thought, "if someone came along and turned *them* upside down? It's not nice. It's not nice at all." And she gave a passing nip to the hand which happened to be holding her.

After that she felt a trifle better.

It wasn't a really hard nip, but hard enough to leave a mark and to show exactly how she felt about the matter.

Then something even worse happened. A large object like a . . . like a . . . Olga tried hard to think just what it did remind her of, descended on her. A hedgehog! That was it. The object looked just like a hedgehog.

For a moment Olga thought Fangio had joined in the attack on her and she wriggled and struggled to avoid this latest outrage on her person.

"Come along, Olga," said Karen Sawdust firmly, as she tried to hold her still. "If you're going to be entered in a show you must have your fur brushed. You want to look your best, don't you?"

Olga felt her heart miss a beat. "Entered in a show! Me? In a show?"

She'd heard about shows from some of the other guinea pigs who visited her on occasion. Some of her friends even knew other guinea pigs who had been in such things. One of them, Charles, boasted of a cousin several times removed who'd actually won a prize, but as no one had ever met the animal in question this was taken with a pinch of oats.

But it made a difference knowing the reason, and Olga lay back and let the brush ruffle through her fur. Really, it was quite a nice feeling. Tingling, but most pleasant, and very good for itches.

"Just wait until I see them next," she breathed, thinking of all her friends. "Just wait until I tell them!"

She went back to her house later that evening looking unusually spruce and well-groomed and with a definite air about her, for it never crossed Olga's mind for a second that she *wouldn't* win a prize.

It wasn't that she was particularly vain, or boastful, or even that she thought a lot of herself. It simply didn't cross her mind.

From the moment she heard she was going to be in a show Olga thought of nothing else.

"I'm being Entered," she told everyone who came near. She made it sound so important that even Noel began to treat her with unusual respect.

And there was so much to do. If she wasn't worrying about where she was going to put her prize—for it might turn out to be a large one—she was worrying over her diet.

"I *must* build myself up," she kept saying. "I *must* eat as much as possible. It's no good looking skinny."

And eat she did. Grass, dandelions, groundsel, clover, paper, cornflakes—Olga was very keen on cornflakes, though she usually only got them on Sundays—oats, anything and everything that came within range of her mouth disappeared in a trice.

And every day her fur was brushed until it shone like the table top itself.

At last the great day came. Olga was up bright and early, and after a final going-over with the brush and comb and a wash of her paws she was on her way.

Mr. Sawdust had made a special carrying cage out of an old letter basket he'd taken off the front door of their house. Emblazoned across the front, in white letters on a blue background, were the words OLGA DA POLGA.

"Of course, the trouble with shows," said Olga once she was settled next to a bored-looking rabbit in a neighboring hutch, "is all the waiting around. I mean they might just as well hand out the prize straight away and let everyone else go home. It would save all this mucking about."

Really it was quite true. For every one person who came and stared at her and then went away again there were a hundred. Some made notes on pieces of paper. Others just talked. Then she was taken out of her box and made to stand on some things called "scales." Goodness only knew why. After which there was a lot of hemming and hawing and more chatter and note-taking.

"Talk! Talk! Talk!" muttered Olga. "Why on earth don't they get on with it?"

"You should know by now," said the rabbit, who was also getting a bit restive, "that human beings *always* talk. They can't even dig a hole in the ground without discussing it first. Not like us rabbits."

But at last the big moment came. The moment Olga had been waiting for. In fact, she was so quietly confident about the outcome of the contest she hardly batted an eyelid when one of the judges stepped forward and pinned something on her traveling hutch.

"Such a nice, intelligent man," she thought, as everyone applauded. "Not that he had much choice, of course, but he did it very nicely."

"Mind you," she mused on the way home, "I'm not saying I wasn't helped by all the brushing I had. Credit where credit's due. But breeding always tells. It's bound to show through in the end."

When she was being put back in her own house and caught sight of a blue rosette on the side of her traveling hutch she grew even more lyrical.

"A rosette!" she cried. "A rosette! Wheeeeee! It's the story of the prince all over again." And she looked round at herself to see if she had grown any more rosettes of her own.

She felt quite disappointed when she found she hadn't. Perhaps they took time to take root.

It wasn't until she caught something in the tone of Karen Sawdust's voice as she placed her carefully back in the straw that a slight feeling of doubt crossed Olga's mind.

"Fancy!" chuckled Karen. "I've heard of guinea pigs winning first prize for having the longest fur. I've heard of them winning first prize for having the smoothest and I've even seen awards for the longest whiskers . . . but *yours* . . ." The voice dissolved into gales of laughter as the door closed. "It just serves you right for being so greedy!"

Olga sat for a while lost in thought. What *could* she have meant? *Me* . . . greedy? What sort of prize *had* she won?

She squinted through the window at the rosette still pinned to the traveling hutch and at the piece of card just below it.

Reading upside down wasn't Olga's strong point and although she had once, ages ago it now seemed, managed to spell out her name when there had been all the fuss about what to call her, new words were much more difficult and the writing on the card took a lot longer.

But then, FIRST PRIZE TO OLGA DA POLGA FOR BEING THE FATTEST GUINEA PIG IN THE SHOW is a lot to get on a very small card, especially when the reader is so indignant she can hardly believe her own eyes.

On the other hand, if it did nothing else it certainly cured Olga of being greedy. At least for the time being!

8 · Olga Starts a Rumor

For a while the next morning Olga felt she hardly dared show her face.

However, a prize is a prize no matter what it's for, and it's certainly better than no prize at all. In fact, it needed only an hour or two outside in her run before she was as right as rain again.

"There's nothing like a spot of sunshine for taking you mind off things," thought Olga. "That and a good doze."

She had several good dozes, partly to avoid being asked too many embarrassing questions about the show, and partly because the excitement of the previous day had left her feeling quite worn out.

In any case she soon had other things to occupy her

mind. They were mostly to do with a round, stonelike object called Graham.

Graham was a tortoise and although he was "known-about" he wasn't often seen on account of his being so slow.

Olga first caught sight of him making his way through the lettuce bed, but what with pausing for an occasional snack and stopping now and then for a rest, it wasn't until midday that he drew level with her run.

"Where are you going?" asked Olga with interest, after they had exchanged a few pleasantries, for her new visitor had such a determined look on his face it was clear he had something important in mind.

"I'm getting ready to hibernate," explained Graham. "We tortoises do it every year. Sleep the winter away—that's the answer. It saves all the bother of trying to keep warm. Nothing like snuggling down under some leaves. It can snow, rain, freeze, do what it likes —it won't bother me."

Olga looked at Graham and then at the sky. Although one or two clouds had certainly come up during the course of the morning and were now casting their shadow over the lawn, the weather didn't seem *that* bad.

"Hailstorms," said Graham. "No trouble at all. Thunder . . . lightning . . ."

"Aren't you a bit early?" broke in Olga. "I mean . . . it's ages yet before winter."

"When you are a tortoise," said Graham, slowly and deliberately, "you need to make an early start. It takes such a long time to get *anywhere*. I have to get up early to cross the road even, and if I want to come back again I have to get up the day before. Still, I shan't worry. Once I've found a good spot, it can do what it likes. Gales . . . drizzles . . . showers . . ."

"But if you sleep all the winter," persisted Olga, who was beginning to get a bit fed up with the weather as a topic of conversation, "how do you know what's going on?"

"Nothing 'goes on,' " said Graham gloomily. "That's something else you discover when you're a tortoise. You go to sleep in the autumn and when you wake up in the spring it's still the same old world. Nothing ever changes."

"Nothing ever changes?" Olga stared at Graham as if she could hardly believe her ears. "*Nothing ever changes?*" she exclaimed. "Why, things are changing all the time."

"Name one thing," said Graham. "Name just one thing that's changed this morning."

Olga gazed round the garden, for once at a loss for words.

"Well?" said Graham. "I'm waiting. Only don't keep me waiting too long. I want to reach the other side of the lawn before it gets dark."

"Er . . . yes . . . mmm . . . well . . ." Olga glanced up at the sky, trying hard to think of something to say, and as she did so a flash of inspiration hit her. It suddenly seemed a very good day to START A RUMOR.

"I don't want to worry you," she said casually, "but did you notice anything funny about the sun this morning?"

"The sun?" Graham turned his head slowly to one side and squinted up at the sky. "I can't see any sun."

"No," said Olga, taking a quick upward glance to make sure it was still cloudy, "and you won't either."

She moved closer to Graham. "It's changed places

with the moon!" she whispered. "It rose the wrong way this morning. Instead of appearing in the east like it always does, it rose in the west!"

Graham chewed this piece of information over in his mind for some time, and then gave a gulp as he at last swallowed it.

"If that's the sort of thing that goes on while I'm not looking," he announced, "I'm glad I'm hibernating," and without so much as a good-by wave Graham hurried on his way as fast as his legs would carry him, until by the middle of the afternoon he'd disappeared into the shrubbery.

By that time Olga had almost forgotten the incident, but shortly afterwards Fangio came rushing across the lawn, his eyes gleaming with excitement and his prickles standing on end like a porcupine.

"Have you heard?" he gasped. "Have you heard? Something's happened to the sun. It's the wrong way round!"

Olga scarcely bothered to look up. "Tell me something new," she said.

"I did hear," said Fangio impressively, "that someone's pulled the plug out of the North Sea. All the water ran away and it's tipped the earth over."

"Really?" said Olga, stifling a yawn. "How interesting."

Fangio looked at her admiringly. "You're taking it very calmly," he said at last. "I must say I wouldn't like to be trapped in a cage at a time like this. I'm going." And without further ado Fangio turned on his heels and ran.

Noel was the next to arrive.

"I know you're not going to believe this," he gasped, "but the sun rose the wrong way this morning. Someone pulled the plug out of the North Sea and all the water ran away. There was a terrible 'glugging' noise. I didn't actually hear it, but they say it was dreadful. And it's all because of the humans. They've been taking all these things out of the earth for so many years . . . coal and oil . . . and gas . . . they've left this great big hole in the middle. That's where it's all gone!"

Noel paused for breath, but if he was expecting Olga to start rushing round her run shrieking for help he was disappointed. She simply went on eating.

"Aren't you going to *do* something?" he exclaimed at last.

"I may," said Olga carelessly. "On the other hand, I may not. I haven't thought yet. I don't believe in thinking too much on an empty stomach."

"Your stomach hasn't been empty since the day you were born," said Noel.

"Well! Well, of all the ..." began Olga.

But Noel had disappeared.

A moment later the sun came out through a gap in the clouds. Olga looked up just to make sure it really was where it ought to be and then she went into the room at the back of the run, closed her eyes, and stretched out luxuriously on the floor.

Starting rumors was rather an amusing way of spending one's day. Not unlike planting a seed and watching it grow before your very eyes. Really, there was no knowing what turn it would take next.

But the turn that it eventually took surprised even Olga.

In fact, it not only surprised her—it petrified her!

It seemed as though she'd hardly closed her eyes before the floor of her run suddenly began swaying in a most terrifying manner. It felt as if her stomach was being left behind while the rest of her rose into the air, twisting and turning, only to land on the ground with a simply dreadful thud.

Olga opened one eye to see what was going on.

Everything seemed all right.

She went outside.

The grass was still there.

She looked up.

The sun . . .

She gave a squeak of alarm.

The sun! *The sun had changed its position!*

When she'd gone inside her compartment it had been on her right. It had definitely been on her right. Whereas now . . . now it was on her left!

"Help!" she cried.

"Wheeeeee!

"Save me!

"I don't want to be the wrong way round!

"Wheeeeeeeeeeeeeee!

"Man the pumps! Women and guinea pigs first. I mean . . . guinea pigs and women! Help! Save me! Wheeeeeeeeeeeee!"

Giving vent to a long and pitiful moan Olga collapsed into a heap on the grass.

"What's the matter?"

"Come along, Olga."

"Good girl!"

The Sawdust family, drawn by the commotion, rushed to comfort her. But it was no use. Olga lay where she was, trembling in every limb, her eyes tightly closed, her feet like jelly. And for the rest of that day nothing that anyone could say or do managed to stir her.

"I can't understand what's come over all the animals today," said Mrs. Sawdust later that same evening.

"There's Noel up a tree, absolutely refusing to come down. Fangio's acting like a scalded cat, and I've never seen Graham move so quickly. Everyone in the road says the same. They're all behaving like March Hares.

"As for Olga . . ."

"It's funny about Olga," broke in Karen Sawdust. "She seemed to be the only normal one until we turned her run round the other way, then she went like it too. What *can* it be?"

But no one ever did discover the answer, and the next day things were back to normal. Noel came down out of the tree, Fangio went back to his insect hunting, Graham carried on looking for somewhere to spend the winter, and all the other animals in the neighborhood went about their business, so in time the matter was forgotten.

But it was noticeable, to those who notice such things, that many of them kept peering up at the sky in a most odd way, and for some time afterwards a certain guinea pig remained very much quieter than usual.

And if there was a rumor going around the district as to why *that* was, it certainly wasn't started by Olga herself. Olga had definitely been cured of starting rumors.

9 · Olga and the "Surrey Puma"

One day toward the end of autumn a crisis arose in the Sawdust household.

Olga pricked up her ears as snatches of it came through the open kitchen window and floated past her house.

It seemed that the whole family had to go away unexpectedly, not just for a day but for a whole weekend. Friday night until Monday morning.

Noel was being looked after by a neighbor, but apparently there were problems over Olga herself—something to do with the time of year and the shortage of grass; a mysterious thing called "not imposing on people," which meant nothing at all to Olga; and THE SURREY PUMA.

There had been talk of leaving Olga with a plentiful supply of oats and having someone call in just to make sure she was all right, but everyone seemed to think she would gobble all the oats up at once, and when the Surrey Puma was mentioned it was generally agreed they couldn't possibly leave her and she would have to stay with relations.

Olga was rather thankful when she heard this last piece of news as she didn't like the sound of the Surrey Puma at all.

For some months past there had been talk of a strange animal which had been seen roaming the area at night, killing sheep, chickens, and anything else it came across.

No one seemed to know quite what it was and the longer it remained at large the bigger it seemed to grow. It was rumored that a young puma had escaped from a private zoo and had grown up running wild in a part of England called Surrey, so in the end it came to be called the "Surrey Puma."

Whether or not it really existed was a matter of great argument, but to be on the safe side many people in the neighborhood began keeping their pets indoors at night.

Noel was one of the few exceptions. He had his own pussy-flap in the back door and was used to coming and going whenever he felt like it.

He kicked up such a fuss when Mr. Sawdust barricaded his private door that he got his own way, though it was noticeable he didn't stay out quite as much as he had in the past.

The evening before she left, Olga went to bed in a state of great excitement. She'd never been away for a weekend before, and when she heard that the "relations" she would be staying with were Karen Sawdust's grandparents her joy knew no bounds.

In fact, she was so excited by it all she scarcely bothered saying good-by when she was collected, but ran round squeaking with delight when her house was lifted into the back of the car.

Her hopes didn't go unrewarded. For it was clear from the moment she arrived that Grandpa Sawdust intended taking his job very seriously indeed.

Scarcely an hour passed by during the course of that first day when he didn't arrive at her front door bearing some new delicacy or other: a handful of grass when none seemed to be around, a carrot or two, slices of runner beans, groundsel and dandelions. Goodness only knew where he was getting it all from, for everyone else's supplies had dried up weeks before.

Olga made short work of everything that was put before her. It seemed a shame to leave anything after he had taken so much trouble. Though by the end of the day even she had to admit that it was perhaps possible to eat not wisely but too well.

"I'd sooner keep you for a week than a fortnight," said Grandpa Sawdust as he arrived with a fresh supply just before dark.

Olga took a deep breath. "And I would sooner stay for two wheeeeeeek-ends than one!" she squeaked happily as she began tucking in.

Though to be truthful by then she was so full that she had great difficulty in crawling from her dining room to her bedroom, and once there it was as much as she could do to open her eyes let alone say good night.

Not that she was able to have her usual good sleep. Instead, a rather uncomfortable feeling in her stomach not only made proper sleep impossible but gave rise to all sorts of queer half-dreams as well. Dreams of finding herself trapped in the middle of a huge forest of thistles and having to eat her way out; of being chased by an enormous wolflike animal with gleaming eyes and razor-sharp teeth, and then being caught in a bog, unable to move her feet . . .

Olga had no idea how long it all lasted—it seemed like hours and hours—but suddenly she woke with a start and the realization that *something really was outside her house!*

She caught her breath as a loud scratching sound came from overhead, and then froze in horror as a large, black shape appeared in front of her window, silhouetted against the moonlight, and looked in at her.

Olga closed her eyes and let out a shriek of terror. "Wheeeeeee!" she shrieked. "It's the Surrey Puma! Wheeeeeeee! Wheeeeeeeeee! Wheeeeeeeeeeeee!"

She shrieked so loudly and at such length that after a while a light came on in one of the upstairs rooms of the big house, then another, and a moment later the back door flew open.

Opening her eyes again Olga saw to her relief that the intruder had disappeared, and she collapsed thankfully into the hands of Grandpa Sawdust as he opened her door and reached in to rescue her.

"What a good job I squeaked loudly enough to frighten it away," she thought, feeling much braver now that she was being carried inside the big house. "Otherwise I might have ended up as a guinea pig with a tale. And not a very nice one at that!"

Olga's stock rose no end when she arrived back after her weekend and told the others about her adventure with the "Surrey Puma."

Animals from miles around came to hear the story from her own lips, and Olga was only too happy to oblige.

As the size of her audience grew and the story was told again and again, so the "puma" itself grew in size.

From being as large as a St. Bernard, it became as tall as a horse, as fierce as a lion, as fleet as a gazelle, and as powerful as a grizzly bear.

She even managed to develop a kind of roar to go with the tale. It was far removed from her usual rather high-pitched squeak, for it started somewhere deep inside and went round her stomach several times, so that by the time it came out of her mouth it really was rather frightening.

Olga's audience listened with bated breath as she demonstrated how she'd used the roar to send her assailant packing.

"I'm not saying it *was* as big as an elephant," she remarked with a certain amount of truth, for even Olga felt she had to draw the line somewhere. "On the other hand I'm not saying it wasn't."

Fangio shivered. "I'm glad I've got prickles," he said thankfully.

Olga glanced at him patronizingly. "I suppose they

might be of *some* use," she said. "But if you can't roar at the same time they won't help a lot." And to show just what she meant she pressed her face against her front door and gave such a horrifying snarl that all the other animals shot off into the night as if they were being pursued by a thousand fiery demons.

All, that is, except Noel.

Having jumped on to the roof of Olga's house for safety, he peered down over the edge and looked at her with interest.

77

"I suppose," he said, "the puma must have come *after* I did."

Olga, who'd been having some much-needed oats after her long bout of storytelling, paused in order to look up, and as she did so a rather odd look came over her face, for there was something very familiar about the shape silhouetted above her.

"I came all the way to see you," explained Noel. "There's nothing much to do these nights, what with all the others being kept indoors, and I thought you might like a bit of company.

"I tried to wake you by scratching on your roof, but I think you were having a nightmare. You kept giving these funny squeaks. Then all the lights came on again so I went back home."

Noel looked wistfully at Olga. "After what you've told us I'm rather glad I didn't stay," he said. "Though I wouldn't mind *seeing* a puma—just once. Tell me about it again."

Olga gulped. "I . . . er . . . there's nothing much to tell really," she said at last. "I may have exaggerated a little I suppose. They're rather like cats. I mean, once you've seen one you've seen the lot.

"Besides," she added firmly, "I've got a bit of a sore throat coming on. It's probably all the roaring I had to do!"

10 · Disaster

Gradually a change came over the weather and Olga began to spend more and more time in her bedroom, only venturing out for meals. She was glad of the board which was put up over her front door every night, for it kept out the rain and the cold winds which had begun to blow. And she was even more thankful to have a window in her bedroom so that she could see what was going on outside without having to go into the chilly air too often.

Now, instead of stamping her hay flat as she'd done during the summer months, she took to fluffing it up and burying herself deep inside where it was nice and warm, and on some mornings, when there was a frost, she even ate her breakfast that way, lying half in and half out of her bedroom.

Then one day a terrible thing happened.

Suddenly, with absolutely no warning at all, some great white balls, large as marbles and hard as iron, came raining down out of the sky, bouncing off the ground and beating down on the roof of her house like a burst of machine-gun fire.

Olga was so frightened by it all she nearly had hysterics. She rushed round and round shrieking her head off.

"Help! Help!" she shrieked. "Wheeeee! Wheeeeee!"

She felt sure it was war and that these were bullets. When she'd first started life in the pet shop some of the older guinea pigs had told terrible stories about the war, and how noisy it had been. None of them had actually been fired at of course, but the stories had been handed down, and like most stories, added to.

At the time Olga had thought it all sounded rather exciting but now that she was actually experiencing war it was an entirely different matter.

"Wheeeeeee!" she shrieked. "Wheeeeee! Help! Save me!"

Somewhere in the background a door opened and she vaguely hard voices calling her name. Then some-one—it sounded like Mrs. Sawdust—shouted for something called an umbrella, and a moment later her door was flung open.

Olga was so terrified by now she simply hurled herself at the opening. Anything to escape from being cooped up in her house, unable to defend herself.

Hands reached out to catch her, but in her terror Olga missed them completely.

She felt herself falling through space. It seemed to last an age, but could only have been a split second, and then she landed with a thud on the wet concrete far below.

For a moment she lay where she'd fallen, fighting to get her breath back. Then, as she went to move, a terrible cold fear came over her, for an awful agonizing pain shot right through her body.

She tried to pull herself along with her front paws but struggle as she might nothing seemed to happen. The whole of the back part of her body seemed to be completely locked. She *wanted* to move, she strained every muscle trying to move, but nothing happened.

Dimly she felt herself being picked up and carried, wet and bedraggled, into a warm room inside the big house, where she was placed in a towel and gently rubbed. But although it was all very comforting it did nothing to ease the awful ache which now seemed to cover her completely like a cloud.

From somewhere—it seemed miles away and yet she knew it must be close by—she heard Karen Sawdust's voice, sounding very tearful.

"Oh, Olga," she said, "what *have* you done? If only you could tell us what's wrong."

Olga struggled against the pain as she tried to lift herself up, but after a few faltering attempts she sank back exhausted.

"Oh, dear," she moaned, closing her eyes as everything around grew misty. "If only I *could* tell you. Oh, if only I could! But I don't even know myself. What *can* it be?"

Olga wasn't sure how long she slept but when she finally woke she found herself lying on a bench in a room she'd never seen before in her life.

There was an odd smell about it; not unpleasant, but somehow rather clean and safe. That was it! It definitely felt "safe."

Mrs. Sawdust was there, and Karen Sawdust, and a man in a long white coat.

The man in white was holding something in his hand, a tiny white object about the size of a groundsel bud, and Olga pricked up her ears as he spoke.

"Give her a quarter of this every day," he said, addressing Mrs. Sawdust. "Just in case she's suffering from shock. That's always a danger with guinea pigs if they've had any sort of accident, and sometimes it takes a day or two to come out. Keep her warm and dry. We don't want her getting any sores—especially as she can't stand up . . ."

Olga listened drowsily as the voice droned on.

Now that she'd been cleaned and dried and had a good sleep she was beginning to feel a little less dazed and the sharp pain in her back had almost disappeared. But it had been replaced by a kind of sleepy numbness, and she couldn't even feel her legs, let alone tell whether they were moving.

Instinctively she knew she was being taken good care of, and that she must do exactly as she was told if she was to get better, but she wished too that everyone would leave her alone so that she could get on with it.

Then she pricked up her ears again as she caught something new the man in white was saying.

"Her back's not broken, and her legs don't seem to be either . . ." Very gently he picked her up and ran his fingers over her body. "There's no sign of any dislocation . . ."

"Oh, dear," thought Olga. "What a lot of things I *haven't* got. I do hope he finds *something* left."

"Bruises," said the man in white. "She'll have plenty of those before she gets better."

Olga suddenly wished she hadn't thought the question. She didn't know what bruises were and she didn't much like the sound of them either, but luckily for her peace of mind she fell asleep again before the vet's next remark.

"We'll give it a week," he said. "Unless there's any sudden change for the worse bring her back to see me in a week's time. Then we'll decide what to do with her . . . *one way or the other!*"

11 · The Dance of the Sugar Plum Guinea Pig

A week went by, then another, and still Olga showed few signs of getting any better.

They were two of the longest weeks she had ever known. Every day she was taken into the big house belonging to the Sawdust family and placed in a basket on the kitchen table so that her legs could be massaged, and every day she was given her tablet and had her fur brushed smooth. As she couldn't bend she wasn't able to do it herself and it soon became terribly matted and unkempt.

The tablet was something of a problem at first. Olga found it impossible to swallow, although it was only a quarter of what was a very tiny one to start with, and the Sawdust family soon gave up the idea of forcing it down her throat for fear of hurting her.

86

In the end Mrs. Sawdust decided to grind it into powder and sprinkle it on her food, so each morning Mr. Sawdust went out with a torch in search of a dandelion leaf.

Olga was pleased about the dandelion leaves. She was quite "off" grass, and as for oats—if she never saw another oat again for the rest of her life it wouldn't worry her, for the effort required to bend over her feeding bowl was too much to bear.

But dandelion leaves were different. Something deep inside Olga told her that of all the food she could possibly have—and in the winter there wasn't a great deal of choice—dandelions were probably best of all.

News of Olga's misfortune quickly spread and Noel began paying regular morning visits so that he could issue bulletins to the others.

Fangio came to see her several times, and once he even brought her a piece of thistle he'd found in the Elysian Fields. But her house was much too high off the ground for him to give it to her, so he ate it himself and after a while went away again.

Even Graham came out of hibernation to see what was going on, and such a thing had never been known before.

After the first week Olga was taken to see the vet again, but he was still unable to make up his mind.

"Tell her to keep on taking the tablets," he said, and then he explained that animals were like human beings in many ways and that sometimes if they'd had a bad fall or something which he called a "slipped disc" the pain was so great that they were too scared to move, long after they were really better.

"Perhaps she needs a change," he said, during their third visit. "Something to take her out of herself."

Olga felt this was much the most sensible remark she'd yet heard. Her present self felt so old and useless and painful that she would have given almost anything to be taken out of it. It would be a pity to lose her fur, of course, especially after all the time she'd spent keeping it clean, but . . .

And then she heard Mrs. Sawdust explain to her

daughter on the way home that what the vet really meant was that Olga ought to have a change of scene, not a change of body, and she became gloomy again.

"What's the use of new surroundings," she thought, "if I'm not well enough to enjoy them?"

However, shortly afterward Olga did get a change of scene. Not a very big one to be sure, but certainly a break from her present humdrum existence.

Each evening when her own house was being cleaned out she was taken into the big house and placed on a rug in front of the living-room fire. Not so near that she would miss it when she went back home, but close enough for her to feel the warmth licking her face.

At first Olga was in two minds about the whole business, especially as Noel was usually around too.

It wasn't that she didn't trust Noel, it was simply a fact of nature that cats can't help chasing anything that moves. But she lay so still on the soft wool rug that really there was no excuse for such a thing happening and in time she began to look forward to her evenings out.

One of the things she enjoyed most was a large box which stood by itself in one corner of the room, for often the front of it lit up and became filled with tiny moving figures, some of whom even *talked*, while often there was the sound of music.

Whenever this happened Olga would stop whatever it was she was thinking so that she could pay proper attention.

Noel explained that it was called a "television." He wasn't very keen on it himself because the only smell it had was a kind of warm, burny one which wasn't very interesting, and once when he'd sniffed it too close his fur had given off a funny crackling sound.

But Olga grew to like the television more and more.

"It's just the thing for invalids," said Mrs. Sawdust, when she saw her look of fascination. "It helps pass the time."

One night Olga was allowed to stay up much later than usual and for some reason the music seemed to her ears more beautiful than any she had ever heard before. Mrs. Sawdust said that it was something called "The Dance of the Sugar Plum Fairy," and sure enough, as Olga watched a fairy did indeed appear, a tiny, silvery figure, floating to and fro in time to the music like a piece of thistledown caught on a breeze.

Sometimes the figure came close so that Olga could see it quite clearly. Sometimes it took fright and ran away again. And once it stood on its toes and spun round and round like a top until it seemed as if nothing could ever make it stop.

For a long while Olga sat entranced, unable to tear

her gaze away from the screen. Then she closed her eyes and in her dreams she, too, began to dance. Slowly at first, and then, as the music grew louder, faster and faster until she felt herself spinning round and round just like the fairy in the box.

"Good gracious!" Dimly, from somewhere miles away, she heard a voice.

"Did you see that?" There was a chorus of excited voices, much closer this time. "Olga . . . you're standing up!"

As the music stopped and the applause rang out Olga opened her eyes and then nearly fell over backwards in astonishment.

It was true! She really had been standing! Not on one back paw as she had been in her dreams; not even on two back paws; but certainly on all four. And what was even more surprising was the fact that it didn't seem to hurt at all.

"I've been taken out of myself!" she squeaked. "I've been taken out of myself at last!

"How nice to be living in such a magical age," she added, addressing the world in general. "How lucky I am to be sure!"

And if Karen Sawdust noticed a row of whiskery faces pressed against the outside of the glass door leading to the garden she wisely kept it to herself. They all appeared to be nodding their agreement, but when she looked again they had disappeared, and there are some things to do with guinea pigs that are best left unsaid. Especially when they've just been doing the Dance of the Sugar Plum Fairy.

It was enough for one evening that Olga was on her feet again.

12 · The Night of the Moon Rockets

Having got back on her feet at long last Olga made a rapid recovery. Her eyes sparkled, her fur took on a new gloss, and she started making the occasional leap in the air, in the way that guinea pigs do when they want to show that all is right in the best of possible worlds.

Not that she was able to leap very far, for the weather remained cold and her outside run had long since been put away for the winter, so apart from occasional excursions into the big house she spent most of the time in her own quarters.

In any case the lawn was almost permanently covered in a blanket of dead leaves and as fast as Mr. Sawdust raked it clean a fresh lot appeared.

Then Olga noticed a sudden change in the routine. Instead of placing the leaves straight on the bonfire, Mr. Sawdust began piling them in a quite different part of the garden, along with sticks, boxes of wastepaper, old tree branches, and goodness knows what else, until he had an enormous pile almost as tall as himself.

Olga was rather pleased about this as she wasn't very keen on bonfires, especially when the wind blew smoke the wrong way and made her eyes smart.

Then, late one afternoon, there was another unusual happening.

It began when Karen Sawdust went into a nearby shed and came out again a moment later carrying a large pile of hay in her arms.

At first Olga thought that her house was going to have an extra-special clean out and she was just getting ready for it when to her surprise Karen Sawdust disappeared from view again.

And that wasn't the end of the affair by a long way.

Some time later she returned carrying what looked like a little old man on her shoulders. She went straight past Olga's house and placed the figure ON TOP OF THE PILE OF LEAVES.

Although Olga hadn't much liked the look of Karen Sawdust's new friend, for he had a red face which seemed to be tied on with string, and was very badly dressed, it did seem a little out of the ordinary to say the least.

But before she had time to dwell on the matter, let alone put any of the two and twos together, Mr. Sawdust appeared on the scene and with the help of his daughter picked up Olga's house, legs and all, and started to carry it away.

"Oh, dear," thought Olga as she swayed to and fro, "I hope they're not going to put *me* on the rubbish dump as well."

But to her relief she found herself being taken round the side of the house and into the large room with big double doors where Mr. Sawdust normally kept his car.

"It's only for this evening," explained Karen Sawdust. "You'll be much safer in here. We'll leave the door open in case Noel wants to come in out of harm's way."

Olga poked her head out from beneath the hay.

"Safer?" she echoed, as the footsteps died away. "Out of harm's way?" She peered up at the garage window. "Dear, oh dear! What's going on now?"

The thought was hardly out of her mind when there was a flash and a whoosh and something shot past outside.

Olga nearly jumped out of her skin, but before she had time to recover from this first shock, there was a loud bang from somewhere overhead and what seemed like a million tiny stars suddenly appeared in the corner of sky she was able to see through the glass.

A moment later there was a scurry at the door and Noel shot through the gap, panting slightly and with his tail between his legs.

"Wheeeeeee!" shrieked Olga. "Wheeeeeee! What's going on?"

"Goodness only knows," said Fangio as he joined them. "If you want my opinion everyone's gone mad. Bangs . . . crashes . . . hums . . . pops . . . rub-a-dubs. My spikes are all of a quiver!"

"Wheeeeee! Wheeeeeeee!" Olga's shrieks grew louder and more desperate with every passing minute as Fangio, his voice punctuated by more explosions from outside, went on to tell of some of the many narrow escapes he'd had before he'd reached the safety of the garage. "Wheeeeeeee! Wheeeeeeeeeee!"

Noel glared at her. "*Must* you make that awful noise?" he asked. "I came in here for some peace and quiet. It's worse than it is outside. You guinea pigs are all the same. Squeak. Squeak. Squeak."

Olga opened her mouth and then thought better of it. "It's better than roaring," she said stiffly. "Or grunting. Or moaning. Or meowing like *some* I could mention!"

"You make it sound as if the world's coming to an

98

end." Noel, recovering from his fright, began to look rather superior as he had a quick wash. He peered out of the window as some more stars burst in the sky. "It's probably only the humans going to the moon again. They're always at it. They go on things called rockets."

Noel was often rather knowledgeable about things in general on account of his getting around a lot and coming across bits of information hidden away in dustbins.

With a great effort Olga pulled herself together. "Guinea pigs," she said, "squeak because they've always squeaked. And as for going to the moon . . ." she paused, not wishing to be outdone by a mere cat, "as for going to the moon, I don't see why the Sawdust people bother. We guinea pigs did it years ago. In fact, that's how we got our squeaks."

Noel and Fangio exchanged glances.

"All right," said Fangio, settling down on an old pile of sacking. "Tell us. At least it'll help take our minds off things."

Olga took a deep breath and closed her eyes. "It was the year One B.D.," she began.

"Don't you mean B.C.?" interrupted Noel.

"I know what I mean," said Olga, getting into her stride. "B.D. stands for *Before Dandelions*, which was a very, *very* long time ago.

"As I think I've mentioned before, there were a lot of guinea pigs in Peru at the time, and food had been getting more and more scarce. Had they known that

dandelions would be discovered the next year they probably wouldn't have bothered, but as it was they decided one day to go to the moon to see if they could find any grass.

"Now in those days there weren't such things as . . . er . . . dockets."

"Rockets," broke in Noel. "It's spelled with an R."

Olga opened one eye and fastened it on her audience. "There weren't any R's either," she said sternly. "They hadn't been invented.

"Anyway, to cut a long story short. Since there weren't any dockets, or R's, or even any ladders small enough for a guinea pig, yet long enough to reach the moon, they did the only thing possible. They stood on each other's shoulders!"

Fangio stared at Olga open-mouthed. "But the moon's ages away," he exclaimed. "It's even farther than the shrubbery!"

"If you really *want* something in this world," said Olga simply, "you'll never get it by sitting down and waiting. But if you go out and *do* things there's no knowing where you'll end up.

"They waited for a suitable night when there was a gap in the clouds and no wind and then they set off.

"First they all stood in a line—shortest on the right, tallest on the left. Then they chose the fattest and the strongest one of all to stand at the bottom.

"Then the next biggest climbed on to his back.

"Then the next biggest climbed on to the second one's back. Then the fourth, and so on and so on until at long last, just before dawn, the smallest guinea pig of all started the long climb up to the top.

"They say it was an awesome sight. Animals from miles around came to watch and to wonder.

"And when word came down that the last guinea pig of all had actually set foot on the moon such a roaring and barking and neighing and braying broke out there were some who thought the world had come to an end.

"It was then," said Olga somberly, "that disaster struck.

"Strong though he was, the weight of all the other guinea pigs had pushed the first one lower and lower into the ground until his head was level with the surrounding turf.

"Suddenly a dewdrop which had formed on a nearby blade of grass rolled off the edge, carrying with it a speck of dust, and landed on the end of his nose.

"He tried to lick it off but his tongue wasn't long enough.

"He tried shaking his head, but he couldn't.

"He tried holding his breath and thinking of other things.

"But it was no use.

"His nose began to twitch, and before he had time to warn the others of the danger he gave the biggest and loudest sneeze you could possibly imagine.

"The huge tower of guinea pigs rocked and swayed most awesomely. For a second or two it seemed as though it might steady itself again, but then gradually a wavy motion set in and began to snake its way upwards. The line started to crumble and a moment later it collapsed and all the guinea pigs fell to the ground.

"Fortunately the surrounding earth was very soft so none of them were badly hurt, but they were considerably shaken and it stopped all their moon plans, for none of them felt strong or brave enough to go through the experience again.

"It was a nasty moment—very nasty indeed."

"It's very interesting," said Noel doubtfully, breaking the silence which followed, "but I still don't see why guinea pigs go 'wheeeeeee.' "

Olga stared pityingly at the others. "You'd go 'wheeeeee,' " she said, "if you fell all that way."

Noel and Fangio looked at each other. "Ask silly questions," said Fangio, "and you get silly answers."

"We've been doing it ever since," continued Olga dreamily. "Our *wheeeeeees* have been handed down. Why, do you know . . ." She opened her eyes, but like the sparks from the fireworks her audience seemed to have faded away.

Olga gave a sigh as she went back to her oats. Taking others' minds off things was really most unrewarding at times. She sometimes wondered why she bothered.

13 · An Unexpected Visit

Olga was in trouble. Not serious trouble, but the kind where everyone else grumbles and you can't do a thing about it and even if you could there wouldn't be much point because no one would take any notice anyway.

It was all to do with her water bowl.

Each morning it was surrounded by a miniature lake, and unfortunately she kept getting the blame for knocking it over.

Olga got very fed up with all the fuss that went on, for only she was low enough to the floor to see the almost invisible hairline crack in the side which was causing all the trouble.

"There are no two ways about it," she decided. "I simply must get rid of it. There'll be no peace until I do."

But when you live in two rooms without so much as a back yard let alone a dustbin, getting rid of things isn't so easy. You simply have to rely on other people, and "other people," being quite unaware of the problem, kept filling the bowl up again.

"I suppose," said Olga sadly, "I shall have to spend the rest of my life tramping around with wet paws. I'll have rheumatism before I'm two most likely."

And then one morning her chance came. For a brief moment she was left alone in her dining room with the front door WIDE OPEN.

It needed only a tiny nudge and the job was done.

The crash brought feet running in her direction. The door was slammed shut and a very relieved voice called out, "Never mind . . . it's only her water bowl. Thank goodness *she* didn't fall out again!"

And Karen Sawdust replied, "At least it's one problem solved. I'll give her a plastic bowl to be going on with and next week I'll put a note up the chimney."

"Put a note up the chimney!" Olga stared through her window in disgust. "What *are* they talking about? *Really!"*

But she soon forgot the matter, for over the next

few days quite a number of equally strange things happened and her mind was awhirl trying to piece them all together.

For instance the very next evening Mr. Sawdust came past her house carrying, of all things, a tree! She definitely saw him carrying a tree.

Then, a few nights later, there was the odd affair of the singing. Right outside her front door!

As far as she could tell it was Karen Sawdust and a group of her friends. It was difficult to make out the words, but it sounded very like "While Shepherds wash their socks by night." It went on for some time, then there was a rattling sound as if something hard was being shaken about in a tin, and this was followed by some whispering sort of giggles as someone called out, "We shan't get much there! Let's try next door."

It was all very puzzling and most of the other animals had similar stories to tell.

Fangio related a fur-raising yarn of how he'd been pursued by an enormous van laden with parcels, which kept stopping and starting in the lane outside, and Noel, whose nightly prowlings took him over a wide area, reported that most of the other houses in the neighborhood had suddenly taken to growing trees in their front rooms, and that not only were these covered with bits of paper and silvery string, but some even had colored lights which flashed on and off.

Egged on by the others he had set off to investigate the one belonging to the Sawdust family, but in trying to catch one of the silver strings in his paw he'd brought the whole lot crashing down and had been banished from the house for the time being.

Olga voiced the thoughts of them all.

"Something," she said, "is undoubtedly GOING ON!"

That very evening, long after it grew dark, there was an even more unusual happening.

Olga was in bed, safely tucked up in her nest of hay,

when someone opened her front door and began *cleaning out her dining room.*

At least, that's what it sounded like. Scratchings, brushing noises, the smell of fresh sawdust being sprinkled on the floor; then a less familiar sound, rather like crackling paper. It went on for some while.

"Oh, well," thought Olga, stifling a yawn, "if they want to clean me out twice a day *I'm* certainly not stopping them."

In any case her bed was much too snug to leave and in no time at all she was fast asleep again.

Whether it was because of all the excitement that had gone on during the past week, or whether it was partly the result of her disturbed night, Olga didn't know, but she slept much later than usual, and when she did finally open her eyes she found to her surprise that the shutter over her front door had already been taken down and the Sawdust family, Mr. and Mrs. Sawdust, Karen Sawdust, and both sets of grandparents, were gathered outside.

Another thing she noticed was that someone had tied a lot of green stuff outside her house—holly, it looked like, for she could see a cluster of red berries.

"Really!" she thought. "Whatever next? There's no sense to it. You can't *eat* holly."

So she yawned and stretched and was about to make

her way through into the dining room to see exactly
what all the fuss was about, when she suddenly caught
her breath and stopped dead in her tracks.

There was something odd about her floor. Odd, yet
strangely familiar. Lines crisscrossing the sawdust.
Lines which looked as if they'd been made with the
aid of a stick. Lines which seemed to make up letters;
letters which seemed to spell out . . .

OLGA DA POLGA!

Someone had written HER NAME in the sawdust. Just

as she had done all that time ago when she had first
come to live with the Sawdust family.

There was something else written below her name
but Olga couldn't be bothered to read it. She ran
round and round the dining room squeaking with excitement, scattering the sawdust as she went.

"You see!" exclaimed Karen Sawdust triumphantly.
"She *does* know what it means! I told you so."

"Yes, dear," said Mrs. Sawdust patiently, "but I do
wish she'd stop running around like that and open her
parcel. It's cold standing out here."

Olga came to a halt. "A parcel? For *me*?"

She gazed round her dining room and there, sure

enough, in one corner was a small object wrapped in gaily colored paper.

Olga liked paper. It seemed a very good idea to wrap a present in something you could eat. But she never really got the chance, for long before she'd taken the scantiest of nibbles the door opened and lots of hands came to help her undo her parcel.

As the last of the paper fell away Olga blinked in astonishment.

"Wheeeeee!" she squeaked, her eyes growing larger and larger. "A new water bowl!"

And then she had a closer look. On the side of it, as clear and round and bright as possible, was written her name.

"You'd better take good care of this one," warned Karen Sawdust as she carefully filled it. "It's a present from Father Christmas and he only comes once a year."

"A present from Father Christmas!" Olga sat staring at her new bowl long after the others had gone.

It was a truly magnificent bowl. It even made the water taste sweeter. And as for washing her feet—by doubling herself up there was almost room to do all four at once!

She could still hardly believe her eyes.

And if the cries of delight which greeted her ears every few moments were anything to go by she wasn't the only one to be pleasantly surprised that day.

Indeed, it wasn't long before Noel sauntered past licking his lips and smelling strongly of fish.

"Merry Christmas," he said.

"Merry Christmas," replied Olga.

Even Fangio had a bowl of milk put out for him.

"What a nice man Father Christmas must be," thought Olga as she settled down in her hay after lunch. "And how clever to know exactly what's wanted." She gazed at the words on the side of her new bowl—OLGA DA POLGA. "Even down to spelling a guinea pig's name. No wonder he only has time to come once a year!"

MICHAEL BOND was born in Newbury, England, and spent much of his childhood raising his own pet guinea pigs. Olga da Polga, however, belonged to his daughter.

He says, "Olga da Polga first came into our lives in August 1965. She was a birthday present for our daughter Karen, and she came from Basingstoke. It all took place much as I've told it—only she cost four shillings and sixpence then, not twenty-two and a half new pence. Quite a bargain really for such an unusual guinea pig. Some of the stories in the book actually happened; others are figments of Olga's imagination. I'm not too sure which are which any more."

Michael Bond, who went on to write other books about Olga da Polga, is also author of *A Bear Called Paddington* and other stories about Paddington. He lives in England.